A Holiday for Noah

written by
Susan Remick Topek

pictures by
Sally Springer

Kar-Ben Copies, Inc.
Rockville, MD

*For my family with much love, and
my students and colleagues for their inspiration.*
—S.R.T. (Miss Sue)

Text copyright © 1990 by Susan Remick Topek
Illustrations copyright © 1990 by Sally Springer

KAR-BEN PUBLISHING
A division of Lerner Publishing Group, Inc.
241 First Avenue North
Minneapolis, MN 55401 U.S.A.
1-800-4-KARBEN

Library of congress Cataloging–in–Publication Data

Topek, Susan Remick.
    A holiday for Noah / Susan Remick Topek; illustrated by Sally Springer.
    p.   cm.
    Summary: Noah enjoys nursery school, but looks forward to Fridays when the Sabbath bread
"challah" is served at snack time.
    ISBN 0–929371–07–0 —— ISBN 0–929371–08–9 (pbk.)
    [1. Sabbath—Fiction. 2. Nursery schools—Fiction. 3. Schools–Fiction. 4. Jews—United States—
Fiction.] I. Springer, Sally, ill. Title.
PZ7.T64417Ho   1990
[E] ——dc20   89–48189
                                                                                        CIP
                                                                                        AC

Published in the United States of America
3 - BP - 12/3/11

Noah loves nursery school.

He loves painting and building and climbing on the jungle gym in the playground.

He loves his friends and his teachers.

Noah goes to a Jewish school. He loves learning about the Jewish holidays and singing Hebrew songs. He especially loves celebrating Shabbat in school.

One Monday morning, Noah came running into his class, shouting, "Is today a holiday?"

"Not today," replied his teacher. "Today we're making Hebrew alphabet soup.

Noah helped make the soup and enjoyed eating it at snack time, but he was already looking forward to the next day.

On Tuesday Noah asked, "Is it a holiday today?" The teacher said, "No, Noah," and brought out puzzles of Bible stories.

Noah chose a puzzle of Joseph's many-colored coat. At snack time he ate a cracker with peanut butter, but didn't ask for seconds.

On Wednesday, when Noah asked, "Is it a holiday?" his teacher said, "Well, today is Sara's birthday, so we will celebrate it at snack time."

Noah sang "Happy Birthday to Sara in Hebrew and English, but didn't even finish his chocolate cupcake.

On Thursday the weather was warm and sunny, and the class played outside on the playground. Noah anxiously asked his teacher, "Is it a holiday today?"

His teacher smiled, but shook her head no, as she pushed children on the swings. At snack time Noah thought the apples and raisins didn't taste as good as they usually did.

The next day was Friday. Noah played quietly. He didn't ask his teacher any questions.

After Israeli dancing in the gym, the children came back to their classroom.

The table was covered with a
white paper cloth. At each
place was a cup of grape
juice. In the middle was a
pair of candlesticks with candles.

Between them were two golden brown loaves of challah covered with a special cloth.

"It's a challah day!" shouted Noah happily.

"Oh, Noah!" exclaimed his teacher. "All week long I thought you were asking about a holiday like Hanukkah or Thanksgiving. But you were asking about Shabbat. You wanted a challah-eating day!"

The children sang the blessings over the candles and the wine. After they sang the blessing over bread, the teacher cut the challah.

She gave Noah the very first slice.

CHALLAH

The word challah (pronounce the ch as in Bach) means dough. This soft, braided white loaf traditionally is served on Friday night, the beginning of the Jewish Sabbath.

Making challah is not hard, but it does take time. Make sure you have a grown-up to help.

You will need:

2 c. warm water	*1 Tbsp. salt*
3 pkg. dry yeast	*2 sticks (½ lb.) butter or margarine*
8-10 cups flour	*4 eggs, beaten*
¾ c. sugar	*1 egg (reserve for glaze)*
	Poppy seeds, sesame seed (optional)

Mix warm water and yeast in big bowl. Add 3 c. flour and all the sugar. Stir, cover, and let rise in a warm place for about an hour.

Put 5 c. flour and the salt in another bowl. Cut in margarine as you would for pie crust, until mixture resembles coarse meal (you can do this in a food processor if you wish).

Add beaten eggs to yeast mixture and stir well. Add flour mixture and work into a ball, adding more flour as needed.

Turn out onto floured surface and knead until smooth and elastic. Put in oiled bowl, cover, and let rise for 2 hours. Punch down, divide dough into parts, and braid. Place on cookie sheet or in oiled loaf pans. Cover and let rise for 2 more hours.

Brush tops with egg beaten with a Tbsp. of water. Sprinkle with sesame or poppy seeds if you wish. Bake @ 350° for 20-40 minutes, depending on size of loaf.

Makes 2 large or 3-4 medium loaves.

(Adapted from *The First Jewish Catalogue*)

A Note From The PJ Library®
Making Shabbat Special

There are as many ways of celebrating Shabbat as there are homes in which Shabbat is celebrated. Common to all celebrations of the Sabbath is the feeling of specialness that infuses this weekly holiday (or, as Noah might call it, challah-day!). Here are some ideas for celebrating the specialness of Shabbat with young children.

✡ During the week, encourage your children to give input about your upcoming Friday evening meal and, at each one's level, let them participate in the preparation.

✡ On Friday afternoon, let every family member know that there will be a sing-along that evening, during which each person may choose a favorite song or two to sing.

✡ Encourage your children to create a special centerpiece for your Friday evening dinner table. Flowers, twigs, a bowl of fruit, a craft project from preschool or home, the beloved family goldfish, or a few recent photos distributed at place settings all make the table appear special while providing a topic for family conversation.

✡ Spend an extra 10 minutes with your children during their Friday evening bedtime routine – read a bit longer, talk about tomorrow's plan for the family, or just cuddle.

✡ Take a Shabbat walk in the neighborhood. Challenge family members to point out something they've never noticed before.

✡ When the weather is in a cooperative mood, get to know your neighbors better. Invite them to come and sit in the back yard or on the porch or deck for a Saturday afternoon chat.

✡ Use this end-of-the-week time to consider with your children what the week held. Did you make a new friend? Did relatives visit you? Did you learn a new game or go down a slide for the first time? An awareness of life's blessings and expressions of gratitude are particularly well suited to the Shabbat experience.